SHADOWS AND SHAFTS

USA TODAY BESTSELLING AUTHOR
V.T. BONDS

Cover design by Get Covers

Dedication

To those who lurk in the shadow, beware. There are some real creeps out there.

Usually, the ones who look innocent have the filthiest minds.

You're welcome.

TABLE OF CONTENTS

CHAPTER ONE

Jennifer

Arousal brought me here. Disappointment will probably send me home.

I grit my teeth and offer Trevor, the guy my roommates are trying to hook me up with, a tight smile. I'd rather push his hand off my lower back and slap him, but I don't want to rock the boat this early in the evening. Later, though, all bets are off.

I meet Becca's eyes and give her a pointed glare. She offers me a pathetic look before glancing at Tia, hoping for back up.

Tia has her new beau's tongue halfway down her throat already. I sigh and shake my head as I tug the hem of my skirt down for the millionth time. This is the last time I borrow from either of their wardrobes. Not only is Tia's skirt way too short for my comfort, but the thin straps on Becca's top keep sliding down my arms, threatening to flash everyone at the slightest shift.

And the cat eared headband is ridiculous, but Becca insisted. At least the headband doesn't dig in behind my ears like the first one she tried to make me wear.

Before I can slide into the booth beside Becca, Trevor takes my spot and gestures to the tiny square left beside him. I almost scoff and sit on the other bench, but Tia's newest fling looks ready to lay her out and fuck her right there.

A dark, heady scent fills my nostrils. Lust heats my veins and adrenaline quickens my heart rate. Like the heaviness before a thunderstorm breaks, the scent kick starts a sense of anticipation deep within my chest.

Trevor pats the bench beside him, breaking whatever trance I fell into. I glance around as I sit, looking for the source of the smell. Perched with half my ass hanging out of the booth to avoid touching Trevor, I fix my top's strap again and fight an unexpected wave of disappointment.

I'll never find the person wearing whatever cologne I just fell in love with.

Trevor wraps his arm around me and pulls me flush against his side, his muscles straining and a quiet sound of distress leaking from him, like it was a chore to move my weight.

I grunt, push his arm off my shoulder, and glare at him as I put space between us. He lifts his hands and smirks, as though that'll diffuse the situation. I open my mouth to tell him off, not at all attracted to his blonde hair and good boy looks, but the waitress sets a laden tray on the table.

"Happy Halloween!"

She doesn't stop, just says the greeting and hurries to the next table.

This club is totally not my scene. Too loud. Too dark. Too crowded. A few people wear masks to celebrate the holiday, but most have on as little clothing as possible. In fact, my black outfit looks absolutely prudish compared to most of the bodies crowding the dance floor.

"Let's toast! C'mon, everyone grab a glass," Chad, Becca's boyfriend of two months, shouts over the music. Trevor tries to hand me one, but I lean past him and take one from the tray.

Goosebumps trail up my spine as a massive, hot hand grabs my ass. As fleeting as the touch may be, it scorches a direct path to my core. Hard and rough, it's exactly what my body craves despite the anger roaring through me. I jerk so hard liquor splashes all over my hand.

"Don't touch me!" I snap, barely holding back the urge to throw the last of the drink in Trevor's face.

My mind catches up to my senses and I realize there's no way that hand belonged to Trevor. It was too big. Too hot. Too strong.

"I didn't touch you."

His hands, resting on the table, hold two shot glasses—the one he tried to offer me and the other he intends to drink. I look around and find no likely suspects.

"Sorry," I all but growl at Trevor and toss back the few drops still in my glass. I snatch the one from his hand, trying to hide how flustered I am.

"Happy Halloween!" Becca lifts her drink, and we all clink our glasses together and repeat her words. Even Tia and her new man deign to take a break from sucking face to toast the evening. The liquor burns down my throat and sets my stomach on fire, adding heat to the simmering need pulsing low in my belly. I set my glass down a little too hard, firming my resolve to find some relief tonight.

Just not with Trevor. The arrogance wafting off him lacks the power I crave. He's just another egotistical jerk who's only trick is a quick one-and-done pump. He'd probably also fist bump his reflection in the mirror afterward. Ick.

Surely I can find someone willing to sate the need in my core, especially in this crowd. I study a few guys showing some promising moves on the dance floor. Maybe I'll accidentally end up in one of their arms. Or maybe both.

Yeah, right, like that'll ever happen. Unlike the heroes in smutty, *why choose* romances, real life men don't like competition in the bedroom.

Case in point, the idiot sitting next to me. He sets his glass down and smirks at me like he's already won me over. I swallow and look away as he shifts another shot glass closer, his intent clear. He wants me drunk and horny.

Depression hovers over me as my mind replays the one time I talked to a guy about my fantasies. He'd been my boyfriend for all of three months—the longest of my abysmally short list of relationships—and his reaction left a scar. His scoff still rings in my ears.

Tia's boy toy moans as she licks his ear. She murmurs something to him before grabbing his arm and standing up. Her eyes meet mine before she yells over the music.

"Let's dance!"

I don't resist when she takes my wrist and pulls me to the dance floor, happy to put more space between Trevor and I. Becca joins us and I dance between my only two friends in this ridiculous town. If it weren't for them, I'd be huddled in bed reading nasty books.

Which doesn't sound too bad right now. Lord knows I've orgasmed more times because of filthy fiction than during sex.

The song changes. Tia steps away and grinds against her beau. As I turn to face Becca, Trevor sidles closer. I shift away from him, my arousal dampening at his interruption.

Becca reaches up and grabs the back of Chad's head to guide his lips to her nape. The sensual sight reignites the heat in my belly. All around me, bodies writhe and grind as people lose themselves to the music.

Massive hands settle on my waist. The tempestuous scent of thunderclouds invades my nostrils. My senses jerk to full alertness as a humongous body presses against my back. I gasp as a thick, hard length mashes along my spine. Wetness floods my panties.

Another pair of hands cup my breasts and squeeze my nipples before disappearing. The body behind me disappears, too.

I blink in shock, freezing like a deer in the headlights. Becca still dances in front of me. Tia grinds against her partner behind me.

Trevor's fingers ghost down my arm, dashing every ounce of my arousal.

Panic grips me. For a prolonged second, my heart refuses to beat before terror sends it galloping into the stratosphere.

"Becca! Something's wrong. I—"

Trevor grabs my wrist before I can touch her and tell her I want to leave. With her eyes closed and Chad sucking on her neck, she dances on as though I didn't just bust a blood vessel trying to scream over the pounding bass. I yank to free my wrist, but Trevor doesn't let go, using his grip to pull me closer to him. The liquor sloshes in my stomach as his front presses against mine. When he wraps his arms around me, resting his hands on my lower back, I think I might actually vomit all over him.

He needs to get off me.

I jam my knuckles into his throat and step away, reaching for Becca's arm, but the couple has moved away. She faces Chad, their tongues down each other's throats as they grind against each other. When I grab Chad's shoulder, he knocks my hand away without lifting his head.

Tia isn't even on the dance floor anymore.

Fear pounds through my veins.

I head toward the bar, praying the bartender will help me. Even if he doesn't, there are other people who can act as witnesses if they aren't too drunk.

The cynical part of me berates myself for being so stupid. People don't come to clubs like this to help others. I mean, sure, maybe someone will understand my subtle cries for help, but Trevor is only part of my problem. Someone might help me get rid of him, but what then?

Who in their right mind will believe me about the two times someone groped me? What the hell am I going to say? That an invisible man grabbed me?

Hysteria rises in me.

Not one man. Two.

Chapter Two

Rajani

The little brunette scampers off to the bar. Sunil follows her, ghosting through the crowd a few paces behind her.

I understand why he's chosen her for our first haunt tonight. She exudes an aura unlike any of the other humans. It's been ages since we've seen such colors clinging to a human's life force. Her soul gives off an energy so tantalizing I want to shove my cock in her right here, right now. The consequences be damned.

She's perfect.

Her screams will be a wonderful boost to Sathanas' power this Halloween.

I can't wait to defile her curvy little body. Her pain will please not only my cock, but my soul as well.

Our power thins. Every year it becomes more difficult to remain connected to both realms, which makes fulfilling our purpose more arduous. With humans corrupting themselves so well, our kind struggle to find suitable candidates to terrorize.

I hate the weakness brewing between myself and my brother. We must properly worship Sathanas this Halloween, the one day a year where the connection between realms is strong enough for us to access our earthly forms, so we remain strong and useful until next Halloween.

The female reaches the bar and waves for the bartender. He nods and tells her he'll be right with her. An annoyed growl grows in my chest as the clingy male from the dance floor slinks up behind her. When midnight rolls around, the human had better be long gone, otherwise he'll find himself in a world of misery.

I would welcome his pain. His hands do not belong on this delicious woman's body. The shimmer of arousal hovering around her dims as he touches her yet again. She elbows him and tries to shuffle away, but the other patrons crowding around the bar block her retreat. She calls for the bartender again, her spine straight and fury emanating from her.

It'll be fun to break this female. She may actually present a challenge, whereas every other human we've targeted broke with little effort. And with her perfect ass and long legs, it won't be any trouble sinking into her over and over again.

My brother slinks through the shadows under the bar, his eyes locked on the petite female as he rises to his full height, standing with the bar top cutting through his shadowy hips. His eyes gleam with interest as he studies her breasts.

My hands itch to feel them again. They fit so well in my palms on the dance floor, and the way her beaded nipples pressed through her shirt tells me her body will writhe in beautiful agony between us.

The human male gets the hint and stomps away. I step closer to the brunette until her hair brushes against my chest. She twitches and looks around. I meet Sunil's eyes and enjoy his predatory smirk.

She senses us but can't see us. Yet.

Time for more fun.

I flip her skirt up, enjoying her deepening blush and the glimpse of her lacy underwear. The curve of her ass fills me with yearning. I want to feel her tight heat squeezing my shaft as I cram every inch inside her.

She pushes her skirt down and darts startled eyes around the room again. I chuckle and grab her ass, loving the way the mound of flesh overflows my hand. Her warmth travels up my arm and emanates into my torso, awakening my senses.

She stiffens and swats behind her, but I don't let go, enjoying her confusion as her hand goes through my wrist. I wait until she turns around with wide eyes before releasing her. The flush on her cheeks and confusion in her eyes ratchets my desire higher, the mix of arousal and humiliation delicious.

She turns and lifts her palm from the counter to wave for the bartender again. I press my front to her back so hard her stomach collides with the edge of the bar top. She grunts and flattens both palms on the filthy surface, pushing back against me and rubbing the underside of my shaft. I bite back a groan and thrust against her, making her jerk and gasp.

She heats my blood as no one ever has before. I'll enjoy pulling every ounce of fear and pleasure from her. Sathanas shall be pleased with the offering.

Her squeak can't hide the growing shimmer of lust in her aura. To the inebriated, rowdy crowd, she looks like any other woman who's had too much to drink. Only myself, my brother, and this tiny female know any different.

Unable to help myself, I wrap my hands around her hips before sliding my fingertips downward. Her scent ripens as I skim the top of her mound, barely brushing her clit through her clothes.

Her attempts to evade my touch prove useless. I shift lower and reach under her skirt. She gasps again as I rub two fingers over the length of her clad pussy. My cock jerks against her spine as I feel how wet her panties are.

Instinct barrels through me, whipping away my control like never before.

I lean down and nip her ear before releasing a growl. Sunil's eyes widen in shock as he stares at her face. I shift to the side and realize they stare into each other's eyes.

My guts clench and I step away from the tempting female.

Chapter Three

Sunil

For the briefest of moments, she sees me. Her eyes focus on mine with a clarity only possible on Halloween, when Rajani and I take our corporeal forms, but we have yet to cross the threshold of the hallowed day. Several minutes remain of Halloween Eve, so she shouldn't be able to see me. The moment my brother stops touching her, she loses sight of me and blinks in confusion. Fear radiates from her, adding more colors to her aura and increasing her beauty. She looks around as she pushes upright, staggering half a step away from the bar and grabbing the edge as though it's a lifeline. Her unsteadiness damns her in the eyes of the other humans. I smirk and shift closer to her.

I want her. Yes, the pull to her delicious presence stems mainly from my inherent need to draw negative energy for Sathanas, but another part of me wants her for selfish reasons.

Rajani grinds his teeth and glares at me.

Our weakening ties to life anger him. He sees no other way besides the unholy script inscribed upon our souls the moment Sathanas created us. I try not to blame him. For centuries, we've known little else beyond the void trapped between realms. On days when the power of Sathanas wanes, we view those on earth scurrying about like insects, unable to interact. It infuriates him.

I understand his musings, except the tiny female before me creates an upheaval in my soul. She feels different. The heat of her lingers on my cock from when I pressed against her on the dance floor.

Rajani already enjoyed her breasts. My turn.

Knowing she has no defenses against me, I pinch her left nipple through her blouse. Her blush deepens and she jerks, lifting her hand as though to stop me. Right before she touches her breast, I release her and pinch her other nipple. Her aura glows with arousal.

A human female knocks into her right shoulder. She nearly falls from the impact. Her squeak of pain as my grip stretches her delicate peak sends magma to the base of my spine. I release her and watch as she responds to the blood flowing back into her nipple. The human male on her other side grabs her shoulder, acting as though she fell into him.

Rage blasts through me. I grab his throat and squeeze. He releases her and scratches at his neck. When I let him go, he staggers backward and sucks in a ragged breath, his eyes trained on the tiny brunette as though a demon just popped out of her skull. He flees. She stares after him, shocked and confused.

I take advantage, sliding her strap off her shoulder and enjoying the sight of her full round breast and dusky pink nipple before filling my palm with her warm, silky flesh. She rushes to fix her shirt even as I twist and tug on her hard peak. Her arousal spikes, scenting the air and shimmering through her aura.

With her tempting flesh covered, she searches for me, her eyes darting around the space in front of her. Tears glisten in her eyes. My hand lifts and caresses her jaw without my consent. She freezes and sucks in a breath, holding it for a long moment before closing her eyes and shaking her head. I pull my hand away. Rajani's scowl deepens.

The bartender yells at our target. She jumps, shakes her head harder, and spins so fast she knocks the female beside her into the group on the far side of the bar.

She flees, stimulating my prey drive. Rajani joins me, evil glinting in his shadowy eyes as we slip through the crowd. Delight spears through me when she pushes through the door to the bathroom. I stop in the hall and turn to meet my brother's gaze.

Our prey cornered itself.

Wicked glee deepens our smirks as we enjoy the thrill of anticipation. Midnight comes soon. We shall enjoy corrupting the tiny female.

Rajani may deny it, but this catch isn't for Sathanas. We may siphon her fear and ferry it to him, but this rutting means more than just another sacrifice.

I feel this in the depths of my soul. She's too perfect to pass up.

She will scream for us. Hurt for us.

And she'll love every moment.

Chapter Four

Jennifer

I push past the two ladies primping in front of the mirror and close myself in the middle stall. My hands shake as I pull my phone out of my clutch and text Becca.

We need to leave.

Now.

The little round icon in the bottom corner doesn't change, telling me she hasn't read it.

Becca I'm serious

help

there's something wrong

I think I was drugged or something

I feel weird

My fingers shake harder as I realize the ladies no longer chatter by the sinks. Silence permeates through the bathroom. A heavy-duty lock clicks. Ice slides down my spine as I realize it wasn't from one of the stalls.

I think I've officially lost it. No one would lock the main bathroom door, not when there are so many people in the club. Stuff like this doesn't happen in real life.

I open my phone keypad and type in 911 with shaking hands, almost dropping it several times before clutching it in my left hand and hovering my right finger over the call button. I strain my ears, searching for any clues that I'm not alone, but the sounds of the club pulse through the walls, so loud I realize no one outside the room will hear me if I scream.

Several minutes pass. Nothing changes. My heart slows as my adrenaline wanes.

Pulling my courage close, I unlatch my stall door and peek out into the bathroom.

When I find nothing out of the ordinary, I step out and head toward the door. My feet falter as dread hits me, my body tensing as my mind replays the vision of a shadowy figure with broad shoulders and an intense stare.

Foreboding settles over me.

I imagined that, right?

The heat simmering in my veins says otherwise. My body yearns for the flare of pain produced by those massive, hard hands pinching my nipples. I've never experienced such raw desire before.

I really must be losing it. This is insane.

I step forward, ignoring the tendrils of pleasure working their way through my abdomen as I remember how the animalistic growl brushed against my ear.

This place must be haunted. Or cursed.

I almost laugh at my crazy thoughts but can't break the sensation of feeling like I'm being watched.

The crowd surges impossibly louder, making the walls shake in time to their chanting. They must be counting down to midnight. I wrap my fingers around the door handle and reach for the lock.

Gigantic arms wrap around me from behind and lift me off my feet. I scream and kick while clinging to the doorknob, desperate to escape even as heat blooms in my core from the heavy scent of thunderclouds. My heart pounds in my head as my heels strike legs so hard pain travels up through my knees.

The dark outline of a masculine hand wraps around my wrist and tugs so hard I lose my grip on the door handle. I look down and realize the arms wrapped around me look the same—void where flesh should be, sucking in the light and creating a shadow in the shape of a man. Fear spikes impossibly higher. My thighs burn and bones ache as I fight against the creature's hold on me, but he hauls me across the room with ease.

I'm too busy fighting to heed the low, ominous note rumbling from his chest when I fling my head backward and clip his chin. He presses my stomach against the counter and gathers my flailing wrists in one massive hand behind my back. I scream and struggle as he wrenches them higher up my spine, sending sharp pain into my shoulders.

His thick erection grinds against my ass. Lust pulses in my lower abdomen despite my mind screaming in terror.

Rough, shadowy fingers wrap around my throat and weave into my hair, forcing my gaze to the mirror. I watch in horror as two sets of eerie eyes stare back at me, menace and lust emanating from them.

They tower over me with shoulders so broad they block out the overhead lights.

Bright purple eyes lower to my level, the creature beside me stooping to press the side of his face against mine. As we stare at our reflections, his smirk widens and he glances at the cat ears before meeting my stare.

"Look at you, little pussycat. Tiny and frail. Terrified and vulnerable. Delicate. We're going to enjoy breaking you. Fucking you. Knotting you."

His deep rumble lights an inferno in my core, even as terror and confusion swirl through my mind. The voice rumbling from his chest sounds so different from the deeper, rockier growl I heard by the bar, but my senses gobble it up like candy and begin an immediate sugar rush through my veins. I hate it.

My body craves more.

I whimper as his hold tightens on my face and hair.

They move as one, yanking me away from the sinks and forcing me onto my knees. I struggle, but my strength can't compare to theirs as they keep tight grips on my face, hair, and wrists. The grimy tiles bruise my knees as the male with purple eyes kicks my legs apart with his ghostly foot.

"Filthy little omega looks good on her knees, doesn't she, brother?" he says as he shakes my head by my hair.

"She's not omega. Not yet."

My insides clench at the red-eyed monster's cruel tone.

"We can remedy that," says the first creature as he releases my face and shifts to stand in front of me with one foot between my knees, pushing my right leg further to the side.

The strain on my shoulders lessens as the other monster separates my wrists, but the relief is short lived. He pulls my arms above my head and captures my wrists in one hand again as he slides his foot between my knees as well, an almost mirror image of his brother.

They stare down at me, lust shining from their neon orbs. Purple eyes fill me with heat while eerie red irises flood my soul with dread. Shoulder to shoulder, they smirk and grab the humongous shafts jutting from between their legs.

No. This can't be happening.

The cold wafting up from the dirty bathroom floor highlights how my panties cling to my soaked labia. Too scared to think, I fight and cry through gritted teeth while clamping my eyes shut.

I'm losing my mind. This is just a hallucination. I got roofied or something. I'm going to get up and walk out of the bathroom. Right now.

The red-eyed monster chuckles and pulls my arms higher, forcing me to rise onto my splayed knees. A whimper escapes my throat, coaxing a moan from the purple-eyed monster. He yanks my head back so far my chin almost points toward the ceiling.

"Be a good little whore and open your mouth."

Brutal fingers pinch the hollows of my cheeks and pry my teeth open as the hand in my hair angles my face toward their hips. Smooth flesh brushes against my lips, but I refuse to open my eyes. Tears pour down my face despite my pulse jumping in delight over their masculine scents. Worms crawl in my overheated belly.

"Look at us, little kitty. Watch us as we fill your belly with our seed," says the red-eyed monster.

I clench my eyes tighter together. He chuckles and slides his foot forward until the front of his leg presses against my pussy.

"Open your eyes or I'll flip you over and fuck your ass."

My heart seizes. A sob wracks my chest. I lift my eyelids. He smirks down at me.

My stomach plummets as he *purrs*. Dark and delicious, his rumble holds promises of pleasure and pain.

The purple-eyed shadow trails the tip of his cock over my cheek and chuckles. The sound holds warped amusement.

"Silly little omega, don't you know never to trust an alpha?" he says, mocking me.

The red-eyed creature digs his fingers deeper into my cheeks and slides the underside of his shaft over my parted lips, bumping my nose with his tip. He groans and meets my panicked gaze as hot liquid seeps from his slit and trails down my cheeks to drip into my hair.

Their massive cocks terrify me. There's no way I'll survive if they shove those things inside my body.

A tiny voice in my head pleads for them to do it anyway. To show me how wonderfully horrible their claiming of my body could be.

His red eyes flare before he narrows them into nightmarish slits. He fits the head of his cock to my parted lips, aiming the stream of precum into my mouth.

As a rush of decadence hits my tongue, his words send me deeper into panic.

"I'm still going to fuck your ass, except this way, you'll beg for it first."

He crams his flange into my mouth, compressing my tongue and forcing my jaw wider. I panic, unable to breathe with my head tilted so far. My muscles jerk and I fight despite the lightning streaking through me from his flavor.

I gasp as he pulls away and rubs his tip against my cheeks and chin.

The purple-eyed monster takes his place, mirth swirling within the intensity of his need. He bites his bottom lip as he angles his cockhead into my mouth and thrusts. I gag as he hits the back of my throat. He shifts away only to cram his broad tip deep into my mouth again.

Magma coats my tongue as he retreats to my lips and leaks his seed into my mouth. As the first drop hits my stomach, euphoria blasts through me. Blinding white light bursts behind my eyes as every cell within my body morphs. A tumultuous hunger grips my belly, demanding satisfaction.

I *need*.

The lust pulsing through me when I left my room this evening can't compare to the magma now boiling in my core. I blink and urge my eyes to focus, terror a close second to my desire.

Dangerous pleasure emanates from their masculine faces as they crowd me. I cry silent tears and fight a battle I know I cannot win as two hard cocks rub against my face and coat me in their precum.

My body turns against me, throbbing and needy.

Two cockheads press against my lips, jerking as they stroke their shafts with their hands.

My vision turns blurry as jets of delectable fluid shoot into my mouth, and without conscious thought, I swallow. And swallow. And swallow.

They don't stop.

Despite my frenzied gulps, their cum leaks from the corners of my mouth and drips into my hair. Their scents invade my nostrils, and I sink deeper under their spell.

I float in a temporary calm, buffered by feral rumbles and suspended by shock.

Is that feminine purr coming from my chest?

They pull away, smearing their dripping slits on my chin.

"Such a good little omega slut. Ready for that ass fucking now?"

My insides clench and the world comes crashing down. I don't want this, despite the need raging through my body. When he releases my face and arms, I lash out.

The heel of my palm slams into the crease of his groin instead of his balls, his brother's fist in my hair ruining my aim. I scratch my nails down his thigh before the hand in my hair yanks me so far back my breath catches. Pain lances up my knees, thighs, hips and ribs as the purple-eyed shadow bends me into an inverted pretzel, my shoulders mere inches from the floor and my eyes trained at the underside of the sink.

"Such a feisty pussycat. I wonder if she'll keep fighting with our knots locked deep inside her body?" The purple-eyed monster murmurs as he hovers over me, his eyes gleaming with depraved interest before he leans out of sight.

"It's been a while since we found a bitch with claws. Yes, she'll fight. I look forward to it," growls the red-eyed shadow.

Even though I can't see them, I sense the difference in their touches. The red-eyed monster peels my panties off my drenched folds with unyielding hands as the purple-eyed creature eases the straps of my shirt off my shoulders with a finger.

With one palm pressed against the floor to prevent them from bending me further, I push and slap and fight to ward them off, but they overpower me with ease. They scratch my thighs and test my hips. Tease my sides and squeeze my breasts. Twist my nipples and grab my throat. All the while, one hand rests at the top of my mound, mere millimeters from my clit, rubbing the surrounding flesh and skyrocketing the lust boiling in my veins.

I dig my nails into the wrist resting above my pussy, pushing and pulling as my body wars with my mind. I want them to stop, but one swipe along my clit will release the pressure building in my core.

When purple eyes lean over me, a squeak of protest escapes my mouth as he tightens his hold in my hair and wraps his fingers around my throat. My panic grows as I realize the dark devil with red eyes owns the hand teasing above the apex of my thighs. Fire licks through me at the silent threat emanating from stormy purple eyes. Delight brightens his features as he glimpses the desire and fear warring within me.

Broad fingers stroke my clit without warning, so fast and hard my diaphragm seizes. I hover on the edge of orgasm, staving it off by sheer force of will. Violet eyes widen in surprise as I grit my teeth over a moan, but I can't process his reaction, too focused on holding onto what little sanity I have left. Two broad fingers delve between my folds. Wetter and more swollen than ever, I scream in painful bliss as the crimson-eyed shadow shoves his gigantic digits into my pussy with such ruthless force I lose control.

My body takes over, clamping down into a destructive wave of bliss as fireworks explode throughout my senses. I writhe and scream and orgasm again as he finger fucks me with abandon, wringing every ounce of pleasure from my body.

It ends in a swirling mist of confusion, my mind dropping into self-loathing while my soul sings with joy and my senses struggle to process my surroundings. I blink as the world shifts around me, everything fuzzy and muted as my heart pounds against my sternum.

When my eyes finally start working again and my nerve endings stop sparking like a broken transformer, I groan in both denial and delight. The red-eyed monster's reflection stares at me as he holds my hips hostage and grinds his cock against my ass, forcing me to watch myself in the mirror. Zings of electricity travel straight to my core, reigniting the flames he snuffed out mere seconds ago.

"Such pretty noises from our little omega slut. Make her scream again, Rajani."

I tense at the purple-eyed monster's words, noting the red-eyed shadow's name despite my heart jackhammering against my ribs. Shivers course down my spine as I glance down and confirm his location. I almost choke on my tongue when I realize how close his face is to my pussy. He props my knees on his shoulders, bringing me higher and making his brother's cock slide between my spread ass cheeks.

A humiliating squeak erupts from my chest, and I jerk away from Rajani's massive cock, only to open myself to the other's tongue. I release the counter and push against his forehead. He chuckles, licks my entire sex with the flat of his tongue, and pierces me with a fiery look.

"She tastes amazing, too. You should sample her before you wreck her ass, brother."

A dark rumble pulls my attention to the man behind me. I stare at his reflection in horror as he sucks his fingers and purrs louder.

"Oh, I've tasted the little kitty. She's ready for a rutting, and I'm done waiting. Cover me in her slick. Now, Sunil, or I'll break her before you get the chance to play."

Sunil ducks down and flicks the tip of his tongue over and around my clit in a horribly effective rhythm while teasing two fingers through my folds. Rajani thrusts his cock against my backside, his fingertips bruising my hips.

My mind replays their names, spewing the titles with hatred while my soul stretches to connect with theirs, a new persona begging to submerge myself in their care.

I hate it, but I'm helpless against their strength. Even their auras conquer mine, inundating my soul with their power. I fight against their sensual imprisonment with all my might, but my struggles result in little more than wiggling: their massive hands hold me in place, vulnerable to their will.

Sunil sinks his fingers into my pussy. Wetness pours from me, covering his entire forearm as he hums against my clit.

An orgasm rips through me, so sudden and brutal my lungs ache and toes tingle. My thighs bunch as he bends his fingers inside me, pressing the soft, spongy part at the front of my channel.

"Ow! No!" Ungodly noises burst from my chest as he smirks up at me and repeats the motion with abandon, driving my body into another explosion.

When I get my bearings again, red eyes hold mine through the mirror. My raw and swollen pussy throbs with emptiness. Sunil's breath ghosts across my clit as he pants in anticipation.

Rajani thrusts his cock between my ass cheeks, smearing the wetness from Sunil's hand all over me. Too overstimulated, I stare back at him with an odd blankness bracketing me away from the world.

Sunil lifts me higher and tilts my hips back, opening me further for his brother. A feminine moan echoes through the room, creating a beautiful counterpoint to their deep vibrations.

My entire body jerks as Rajani's broad, smooth cockhead slides through my labia. He grins and settles the length of his cock over my groin, bumping my clit with his flange. I glance down and suck in a breath at the visual delight. Sunil's chin almost brushes the tip of Rajani's cock as it thrusts from between my legs.

There's no way that will fit inside me.

He pulls his hips back and slides the top side of his cock along my splayed folds several times, building my trepidation and coating his shaft with the slick pouring from me. The feminine voice sounds again, higher in pitch as part of his shaft expands and bumps along my tender flesh.

I don't know what the fuck that is, but if it makes him bigger, then there's no goddamn way I'll survive this.

He shifts his hold on my hip, his fingers wrapping around my upper thigh until his nails dig into the lower curve of my ass. I tense as he fits the head of his cock to my asshole.

The odd floating feeling breaks. I scream and fight, angry at myself for not being stronger and fueled by the knowledge of my certain death.

Dark greed shines from red orbs. Sunil's hands part my ass cheeks even farther apart.

Rajani drives his tip deeper into my unwilling body. Fire burns through me as he stretches and stretches me. Dormant nerves light up and join the dark, pulsing need in my core.

My mouth opens on a silent scream as he slowly, ruthlessly, buries his shaft inside me. The world spins as I strain for relief, a hysterical part of me wishing he'd cram himself in fast and end this torture. Surely, if he took me in one swift motion, I'd die and be done with this nightmare.

With unyielding power, he feeds his gigantic cock into my virgin asshole until his groin presses against my backside. Drowning in dark lust, I struggle at the feeling of fullness. My entire abdomen throbs, and my asshole sends streaks of lightning through my body every time he shifts.

"Beg me to stop. Tell me you can't handle it," Rajani demands.

I can't breathe. Any movement results in terrifying sensations.

A chuckle from between my legs splinters my control. Tears roll down my face and blood fills my mouth as I bite my tongue.

I swallow and clamp my teeth together as Sunil swipes the flat of his tongue along my sex. When he drops my feet to the floor, I moan in pain as the massive shaft moves deep within my body.

Rajani slips backward and surges back in, barely moving and yet wrecking me. I cough, blood from my bitten tongue splattering on the counter and dribbling down my chin.

My tormentors freeze. A tense moment passes. Their growls resume, deeper and rougher than before. Sunil grabs my throat and rises in front of me, breaking my death grip on the edge of the counter. Rajani tortures my ass with another small stroke of his cock.

Sunil hooks my knees over the crooks of his elbows before closing his fist around my throat again. Rajani's digits dig into my ass, their sheer strength keeping me held aloft. Trapped between them, overflowing with agonizing pain, I choke on my blood and fight for freedom despite knowing my efforts are useless.

Another smooth, wide cockhead presses against my intimates. Panic spears through me. Blood seeps from my lips, trails down my chin, and paints the back of Sunil's shadowy hand.

"That's right, keep fighting. Such a good little omega. Our beautiful little slut."

Sunil's rocky words flip a switch inside my body. Pain morphs to pleasure so intense I lose myself for the slightest of moments, filthy thoughts drowning me in lust.

He thrusts his hips and impales me on his goliath cock.

The world erupts into a kaleidoscope of colors, fragmenting and splicing the millennia together until time becomes a jumbled, incoherent mess. Every cell in my body rejoices, dies, and comes back to life with each passing millisecond.

"Fuck, she's tight," Sunil moans as he leans back against the counter and squeezes my throat. My skull tightens around my brain.

"Too tight," Rajani snarls from behind me. His bare chest rubs against my back, scorching my hypersensitive flesh.

"It's been too long," Sunil says through gritted teeth as black spots dance along my periphery.

Rajani's finger strokes lightly against my hip, the touch so gentle and full of awe my heart stutters. His deep, rumbly vibration sends tremors up my spine as he hums in agreement. My brain can't handle the dichotomy. The brutal, menacing male who forced his cock into my unwilling asshole can't be capable of such reverence.

"You picked the perfect little whore to wreck. Stop talking and give her what she deserves."

His words rip my hope into tiny shreds. As a fresh tear slips from my lashes, the universe shrinks to the two cocks pummeling in and out of my body. I shriek and fly apart, blubbering and orgasming, turning into a feral beast incapable of logical thoughts. My nails tear at shadowy flesh and my temples throb as Sunil's fist tightens and loosens around my throat with every thrust.

At the height of euphoria, I meet purple eyes and lose pieces of myself I never knew I had. His glowing orbs demand more, embedding themselves into my psyche and changing everything I thought I knew about myself.

Their grunts are my only warning.

As one, they jam their cocks as deep into my body as possible, their hands pushing me down and pinning me right where they want me.

Their bruising holds aren't necessary. Portions of their shafts balloon inside of me, rearranging my insides and locking their dicks in place. Unable to breathe through the pain, blanketed by roaring lust, I shatter into a trillion pieces. Sunil's expansion compresses my G-spot, tossing me over another cliff while Rajani's swollen shaft stretches me to the brink of endurance. Tumultuous currents of pleasure sweep me up and down, until direction has no meaning.

When my body stops seizing in horrible euphoria, I become a boneless heap in their arms, trapped between their hard bodies and locked on their engorged cocks.

Sunil's hand slips off my throat, tracing my collarbone and teasing the upper slope of my breast until the pad of his finger swirls dangerously close to my nipple. When he circles the softening peak, heat surges through me and blood rushes to the sensitive flesh.

He pinches me. My back arches. Their cocks shift. I explode again, my tired organs responding with such gusto I shake my head before falling limp again. Rajani groans and pulls me back against his front, sending me into another fit of release.

"Such a good little omega, coming all over our knots like the slut she is. Hells, if she keeps coming like this, our knots may never deflate." Sunil's words hit me like a freight train.

Knots. I'm tied to them by their engorged shafts. They forced me between them, crammed their cocks inside me, and now we're stuck together. In a bathroom. On Halloween.

How long will they torture me?

Fresh tears spring into my eyes. I don't have the energy to stop them. They flow down my cheeks unimpeded, joining the dried trails of blood from my bitten tongue.

Rough digits pinch my chin and turn my head, forcing me to meet red eyes. Weight pulls on my straining organs as a wave of release spurts from his tip. His features tighten before he smirks and speaks in the most gravelly voice I've ever heard.

"I love the feisty ones, and she may be the feistiest female we've ever hunted. Her anger makes me want to rut her again, even though I'm still locked deep inside her."

His praise fills my soul with glee, but I stomp it out with my humiliation. Instinctual pride rises next, encouraged by his satisfaction, but I snuff it out with my anger. Longing flows through me at the softness emanating from his eyes, but I flatten it with sheer force of will.

His eyes widen as he searches my face, surprise spreading over his features almost in slow motion.

I want to destroy them the same way they've destroyed me, but I know it isn't possible. My only hope is to get away as quickly as possible and forget this ever existed.

I can just pretend this was a horrible nightmare, right?

Sunil tweaks my nipple and fragments my hope into tiny shards.

CHAPTER FIVE

Rajani

Over an hour passes as we torture the little omega trapped between us. I lose myself to the pleasure, enjoying the tightness of her ass and her responsiveness to our touch. Her pheromones drown all other scents, capturing my attention again and again. Several times I stop myself from bending forward and burying my face in her nape, knowing my resolve won't hold.

She stole something from me. I do not want a mate, yet the urge to sink my teeth into her flesh plagues me.

A mate only denies Sathanas his rightful worship—The Keeper of Halloween thrives on the fear and pain of those suffering on the holiday. He needs as many victims as possible, which means we must finish with this omega and move on to the next human.

The thought holds no appeal. I grit my teeth and close my heart to all outside stimulation, refusing to acknowledge the sliver of a link tying me to the female. There's no way this weak little thing will prevent me from doing what Sathanas created me for, no matter how luscious her curves are or how beautifully she took our cocks.

And especially not the intermittent emotions sparking from her eyes.

In all our decades of tormenting humans, we've never found one with an aura as strong as hers. Even now, with her abdomen swollen from our cocks, knots, and seed, her aura swirls with color. Most females either lose themselves completely or dim to a dull grey the moment our knots inflate within them.

I want to stay locked inside her tight heat forever.

Which is why I grab her hips and pull away despite my still inflated knot. Another release bursts from my tip as she squeaks in distress, but I push through the pleasure and wrap my right hand around her nape. Pinning the side of her face to Sunil's chest, I slap her already bruised and flushed ass several times to prove how little I feel about her.

Maroon leaks into her aura, indicating a fresh wave of emotion roiling within her, but I keep the barrier between our hearts and watch with detached fascination.

"Beg me not to, little kitty."

Her brows scrunch at my words. I chuckle, enjoying how addled our cocks make her.

"Open your pretty little mouth and beg me to keep my knot in your ass, otherwise I'll pull it free right now, while I'm still fully engorged."

Expecting her to either tighten in fear or start crying, she surprises me by clenching her teeth and glaring over her shoulder. I add more pressure to her nape, smooshing the side of her face harder against Sunil's chest.

The urge to fall to my knees and worship her strikes me so hard I lean forward. When the heat of her nape hits my lips, I rear back and snarl.

Her allure seals her fate. She deserves to hurt. No female will sway me.

"So be it. Remember, you could have stopped this. This is your fault."

I tilt my hips away from her. She doesn't make a sound despite the pressure of my knot as I prepare to yank it free of her ass.

Sunil's fingers close over my wrist. With his lips in a tight line and fury shining from his violet irises, he looks ready to tear me to shreds. I grit my teeth and raise an eyebrow, daring him to deny me my right to hurt our latest conquest.

Sathanas demands worship. I am merely doing what our Keeper created us to do—terrorize puny humans.

He pushes my wrist as though to pull my hand away from the female's nape. I scowl and tighten my grip on her. She trembles between us, earning herself more of our seed.

Her silence as I tug my engorged knot against her insides mocks me. I will ruin her.

My hips refuse to move. I dig my nails into her ass cheek and grind my teeth together while narrowing my gaze on my brother.

This is wrong.

I can't wreck her perfect body, but I refuse to back down, so I release her ass and reach between my legs. Closing my fist around my balls, I squeeze until pain shoots through my entire groin. As my knot softens, I twist my wrist and snarl.

When my knot deflates about halfway, I grab her ass and yank away.

She screams.

I win.

The victory proves hollow.

Regret plagues me. I struggle with the foreign emotion.

My body moves as though orchestrated by someone else. I stroke down her spine and fill both palms with her ass. Grinding the underside of my cock between her cheeks, I watch as my seed spills from her, coating our legs and puddling on the floor. She stays tucked against Sunil, the side of her face mashed against his chest and his knot locked deep within her.

A purr unlike any I've ever made vibrates from my chest. When I understand the notes of comfort woven within, I stop and scowl at my brother's unhappy expression.

My feet carry me away from the tempting omega. I swipe handfuls of paper towels from the dispenser and twist the faucet on. Turning to stare at her squished, blotchy, tear and blood caked face, I force my heart to stop ricocheting around my chest.

Sunil's scrunched brows mirror my confusion.

I don't know what prompts me, but I wait until the water steams before dunking the paper towels under the spray and wringing them out. My thumb traces across her cheekbone as I step back around my brother's side. I drop to a squat behind her and press the first paper towel against her red, swollen asshole.

No crimson trails down her inner thighs, showing both my restraint and her body's acceptance of our seed. I gentle my hands, cleaning her with the apology I pretend I do not need to make. She tenses and trembles, her body too sore and abused to enjoy my attention, no matter how light my touch.

Hidden from my brother's prying eyes, I allow my lips to lift in a small smile. Her shapely legs look amazing wrapped around Sunil's hips, his cock still lodged deep within her body. I can't help but use the next paper towel to tease around her swollen labia, making them both groan as I brush their joined flesh. Fresh seed splatters onto the ground, but I ignore my kicking shaft and drop the used towels.

I move down her thighs with gentle strokes and clean Sunil's legs with rougher swipes. Taking the last towel, I return to her ass, circling the red and puckered hole before folding the towel and cleaning the tempting curves surrounding it. Dark purple bruises, roughly the same size as my fingertips, form on her hips and ass, and a deep flush denotes where I spanked her. Dropping the paper towel, I frame her round ass with my hands and nuzzle my face against her left cheek in a tender caress.

Longing fills me. I want to worship and pamper and ravage her.

Her utter stillness ends my lapse of judgement. I turn my head and bite her abused flesh, not breaking skin but hard enough to leave a bruise. Her low moan holds a hint of arousal despite the anger flashing through her aura.

I stand and separate myself from her for the last time, determined to put as much distance between myself and this beguiling female as possible.

She will not trick me into losing sight of my purpose. My efforts belong to Sathanas.

And so does Sunil's.

Chapter Six

Sunil

Rage roars through me. My link to my brother sits like a block of ice in my chest and his eerie red eyes are as closed off as the bond between us.

He's lost. Trapped between our need to serve Sathanas and the truth.

There's something special about this omega, something I can't describe. She has her own gravity. It pulls me to her. It pulls him as well, but he refuses to see her for the gift she is.

For decades, we've heard rumors of other Halloween alphas finding their mates. At first, Rajani listened with neutral thoughts, but as time passed, he grew to hate the concept.

He turns and walks to the other side of the room, propping his shoulder on the divider between the stalls. His expression fuels my fury.

The female in my arms sags despite my knot jerking within her. I align my forearm with her spine and hold her against me, struck with awe at how perfectly she fits in my arms.

Exhaustion keeps her pliant as I stroke her hair away from her face and draw lines down her side. Her flesh pebbles and a tiny shiver courses down her body.

I groan and tilt my head back, leaning more fully against the counter.

Rajani snarls and crosses his arms over his chest.

"You waste time. Finish," he demands with a sneer.

Her belly presses against me. Even with the intrusion of my brother gone, her body cannot handle more of my seed.

It's for her sake that I turn, set her ass on the counter, and prop her in the corner. She shakes as I remove my arms from around her, pain tightening her expression. The colors of anger, humiliation, and fear swirl within her aura, almost coaxing me to torment her breasts and prolong our joining.

I brace my palms on the filthy walls, my right wedged between the paper towel dispenser and my left on the mirror, and glance down at her one more time before closing my eyes.

Her dainty features will never fade from my mind. I want to conquer, destroy, and praise this female with my every breath for millennia.

I don't know her name. I don't need to know her name. My soul longs to connect with hers, despite the barriers between us. Her anger shimmers around her like a shield, barely keeping her psyche strung together.

Her strength amazes me.

Rajani rumbles a warning.

I drop my forehead to rest on hers for the briefest of moments before tossing my head back and focusing on deflating my knot.

As a creature of evil, my thoughts immediately highlight dark memories, which harden my cock. I groan before dropping my right hand to my balls and squeezing.

Opening my eyes, I meet my brother's reflection in the mirror, using my annoyance with him to speed the deflation of my knot.

With an inaudible pop, I lose purchase within her. Thick liquid gushes from her pussy as I yank my cock away, coating the counter, flooding into the sink, and dripping onto the floor. The deepest purr I've ever produced rumbles from my chest.

The urge to lean down and seal my mouth over her pussy punches me in the gut, but Rajani's fingers clamp around my bicep, halting my momentum. Instead of fighting against him, I lower my other arm from the wall and swirl my fingers along her splayed thighs. She doesn't move, lying propped in the corner and staring up at me with round, vulnerable eyes.

I can't help it. I run my digits through her abused, weeping folds before spreading them to reveal the bright red, semi-swollen nub of her clit. It glistens in the light, drenched from her slick and my seed. I circle the sensitive flesh once and fill my nostrils with her pheromones, praying for control.

Peeling my eyes away from the sight of her hurts, but I meet Rajani's face through the mirror.

My shaft throbs in need again already, bumping against the edge of the counter and sending a stream of viscous fluid to the floor.

She tenses and shifts but has nowhere to go. Her hands brace behind her hips, preventing her from sliding forward, but my body blocks her only escape. Exhaustion steals her bravado, her arms shaking so badly her back rattles the mirror. Pleasure flows through me as her clit hardens and lust colors her aura.

Instead of stroking over the needy bundle, I sink my digits into her body, wanting to watch her expression as I push my seed back into her, but staring my brother down instead.

I return Rajani's scowl and pump my fingers in and out of the tiny female, loving the silky, wet heat of her tight cunt.

"Stop, Sunil. It's time to find a new bitch to torment."

"No. I'm not done with this one."

His fist collides with the side of my head. My digits slip free of the tiny female's pussy as pain blasts through my skull. I retaliate before my senses right themselves, fury powering my punches. We brawl, swapping between corporeal bodies and shadow form, splintering the partitions and breaking the toilet bowls.

On the other side of the walls, the party continues, every human—except the one we wrecked—blissfully unaware of our existence. I accept my brother's desperation, pain stabbing through me as he lands savage blows, his evil cunning on par with mine. We release our frustrations on one another, neither of us willing to admit defeat even as glass rains down from the broken lights, tiles shatter, and pain radiates from our shadow forms from ripping chunks out of each other.

When there's nothing left in the room to destroy besides the sink and mirror, we separate and stand on opposite sides of the decimated stalls, our chests heaving and flesh torn. Water fountains up from the ruined toilets.

"You will not mate with her again," he says, breaking the relative silence.

"Yes, I will."

"You cannot! We will find a fresh sacrifice and you'll forget all about this one."

Pain pulses through my face as my scowl deepens.

"No, I will not forget about this one. I want to take her again and again. I want to knot her all Halloween long."

"You speak of betrayal. Sathanas depends on us."

"Does he, though? Tell me, brother, what is our reward for obeying him?"

Rajani does not answer, his jaw shifting as he grinds his teeth together.

"We've been faithful for decades yet fade with every passing year. Our reward? Death."

His fists tighten at his sides, but still he does not answer.

"If I shall die, then I will enjoy life while I have it. I want to fuck her again and so I shall."

He grinds his teeth and narrows his eyes before responding.

"You will not."

"Who'll stop me. You?"

"Yes."

I throw my head back and laugh.

"You'd rather waste Halloween brawling with me instead of admitting you want her. You are pathetic."

"I don't need to fight you all Halloween. I have won."

With dread climbing up my throat, I follow his gaze across the room.

Juices puddle on the counter, but there's no omega in sight.

She escaped.

CHAPTER SEVEN

Jennifer

My knees wobble and legs shake so hard I can barely stand, much less weave my way through the crowd, but I shoulder onward like I have no choice.

Because I don't. I won't survive if they catch me. I don't know how I'm still alive.

There's no way I can escape them. I know that. It's obvious, but I can't admit defeat.

I hurt yet don't feel anything. My insides throb and a sharp ache spears through my groin with every step I take. Determination keeps my toes pointed toward the front door. My shirt won't sit on my breasts right. Probably because I put it on backward.

My brain flips from hypervigilant to floaty. One moment, I see every speck of dust in the air, the next I can barely make out the shapes of people around me.

Shock. I must be in shock.

The car. Get to the car.

No. Call a cab.

What do smart people do?

A giggle bubbles up from my chest, the idea that I might do something smart ridiculously hilarious.

I reach the entrance and realize I don't have my purse.

Of course I don't. I barely remembered to pull my skirt and top back on.

With my hair matted and slime coating the inside of my legs, I wobble toward the bouncer and open my mouth to speak. A shriek from outside grabs my attention. The bouncer's bushy eyebrows scrunch, but my body already faces the familiar voice and there's no way I can force myself to retrace my steps.

I need to get as far from here as possible.

Stepping out onto the sidewalk, the chilly fall air pebbles my exposed flesh. I wrap my arms tighter around myself and head toward the voice as it shrieks again. When I turn the corner toward the parking lot, I spot my roommates staggering through the parked cars. Tia and her man, who seems almost effeminate compared to the monsters I just fled, support each other as they weave toward the back corner of the lot. They've already passed the car. Neither seems capable of standing on their own.

My eyes latch on to Becca. She screams and waves her arms around, anger in her every gesture. I can't focus on her words, but she stares at her boyfriend, who's name I can't remember, and stomps her foot.

Despite supporting myself on every car as I pass, none of their alarms go off, and by the time I enter the illuminated circle from the parking lot's light pole, an odd calm falls over me. Nothing matters except getting home. I can lock the door to my room and pretend like none of this ever happened. I can. I will.

Becca finally notices me.

"Where have you been?!"

The accusation in her tone throws off my balance. I catch myself on the hood of her car.

"I want to go home."

Hoarse from screaming, my voice hardly sounds like my own, but the words emerge with relative ease since I mean them with my whole heart. At least, I think I mean them. I refuse to acknowledge the part of me whining to turn around and find the creatures who cracked my heart in two and pushed their way inside.

They assaulted me. Hurt me. Did things I didn't want them to do.

Yet I can't say the r word. My brain refuses to classify what happened in the bathroom as rape. The grime and fear clinging to me tell otherwise, but my soul feels lighter than it ever has before and my body vibrates with satisfaction. I never imagined pleasure could be so extreme.

"Well, you get your wish. Andrew got us kicked out for doing drugs," Becca yells so loud I cringe.

I draw a blank on the name Andrew until Tia and her boy toy stagger into the light. Right, Andrew is the guy Tia's been necking all night.

"You got kicked out."

I don't know why I repeat her words. Maybe my mouth somehow knows she needs me to respond to her.

"Yeah, because of him!" Becca swings her arm at Andrew. He grunts as her palm smacks against his sternum.

"Not my fault. Not my drugs. Planted," he says before bursting into laughter.

"Shit, he's high as a kite. Take us home, Becca. Please," Tia begs, and I realize she's high, too.

Becca sighs and opens the back door. Andrew dives in while Tia thanks Becca in stilted gibberish. I step forward to join them, but Becca slams the door. When I shuffle closer, I see the couple already attacking each other, their lips locked and clothes half off as they spread over the entire back seat.

"You can ride shotgun," Becca snarls as she reaches for the passenger side door. She fumbles several times before cursing and yanking it open.

"Shit, I'm so mad I'm shaking. I don't think I can drive. Your turn." She holds the keys out to me. I blink at them, wanting to take them with every fiber of my being, but my arms refuse to uncross from my chest.

"I can't drive, either." The words stick on my tongue. I fight to stay upright as the concrete sways.

Becca's boyfriend, whose name I still can't remember, shoves her into the passenger seat and takes the key from her.

"I'll drive," he snaps and moves as though to close the door. Becca grabs the handle and holds it open.

"What about Jen?"

"She can call a cab."

I blink, the memory of him pushing my hand off his shoulder on the dance floor flashing through my mind.

"I lost my phone."

"You lost your phone! That's not like you, Jen," Becca says, her focus narrowing on my face for the first time. I swallow but don't turn away, desperate to hide the hollowness forming inside me but knowing I need her help.

"Use Trevor's phone," Becca's piece of shit boyfriend says while reaching in to pull my best friend's hands away from the door.

Like a cockroach crawling out from under furniture, Trevor appears at my side. Annoyance slides down my spine.

"No. Let me borrow your phone, Becca," I say, panic creeping back into my faux calm.

She swats her boyfriend's hands away, snaps open her purse, and hands me her phone after unlocking it.

"Turn off the password feature while it's unlocked. Call a cab. Use my payment info if you need. Call Tia if anything happens. I'll grab her phone when we get back to the dorm."

I clutch her phone to my chest and watch as her boyfriend slams the door and rushes to the driver's side. I still can't remember his name.

Before he turns the car on, I dial for a cab.

Trevor cups my elbow and guides me away from the parking spot. My fingers shake so hard I struggle to press the call button, but I force my attention to the screen and press the phone to my ear.

My body works on autopilot, responding to the operator's questions and putting one foot in front of the other. When I hang up, I pull the screen in front of my face and fumble through the settings until I know it won't lock me out.

I have no pockets to stuff it in, but even if I did, I wouldn't. My fingers refuse to loosen around the hunk of metal, my jangling nerves focusing on it like a lifeline.

"How long until pick up?"

With a start, I realize Trevor still holds my elbow.

"Let go of me."

I fight down bile as tar spreads through my veins from his touch. Whereas before his attention felt creepy and annoying, now I hate it to the marrow of my bones. I loathe it.

He keeps strolling along as though I didn't speak.

"When will the cab be here?"

My senses snap to alertness as I register the bricks surrounding us. He led me to the alley behind the club. Music pulses through the wall and a stack of trash bags sits at the mouth of the alley.

"It's probably already here, so let me go."

I honestly don't remember any of the conversation I just had over the phone, but I need him to go away. In a last-ditch effort to give him the chance to release me, I wait half a second before digging my heels in and pulling back.

He hauls me around the corner into an even smaller, filthier alley. Before I can suck in a breath to scream, he pushes me against the wall and covers my mouth with his hand.

I scream and bite his palm. The taste of copper makes me heave. His other hand roams over my body, increasing my nausea. He grinds his front against mine, mashing my back into the bricks. Pain lights up my exposed flesh as the rough surface scrapes my skin.

I fight with everything I have, but he's stronger and bigger than I am, and someone else has already cleared the path for him. His sweaty palm glides up my thigh, aiming for my naked pussy.

"Stop fighting. It's obvious you already fucked someone. Just let me have a turn, then you can go home," he mumbles in my ear, his breath haggard from struggling with me. His arms bleed from my nails, but he shuffles closer, using every ounce of his strength to keep me pinned to the wall. I can't reach his face or his groin to incapacitate him.

"Or do you need money? Isn't that what whores like you want?"

Bile rises in my throat as his digits work their way between my clenched thighs. My soul shrieks in despair. This feels nothing like what happened in the bathroom. No pleasure buffers me from his cruelty.

Despite his hand partially covering my nose, I fill my lungs and bite his palm even harder.

He yells and yanks his hand away but slaps me, ending my scream a split second after it starts. My head hits the wall so hard stars dance across my vision. His fingers spear into my pussy.

Underneath the sounds of our fighting, an ominous note fills the air.

Trevor flies backward and crashes into the far wall of the alley. A black shadow descends around him. He screams. Blood sprays in all directions.

The shadow morphs into a gigantic man with red eyes. Rajani.

My knees give out. I crumple to the filthy ground, earning myself new bruises.

Trevor's blood continues to spray across the alley. I cringe as crimson liquid splatters onto my legs.

All traces of adrenaline drain from me, but my mind screams for me to run, so I point my face toward the alley and start crawling. Broken glass pierces my palms and knees, but I keep going.

An arm wraps around me and lifts me from the ground. I grunt as my back smacks against the wall again.

Glowing red orbs steal the rest of my breath, Rajani's fury terrifying me beyond measure even as my skin leaps at his touch.

"You let him touch you?"

I don't understand his rage. At all.

His massive hand closes around my throat and pins me to the wall. My hands lift on reflex and wrap around his wrist.

"Not even two minutes after we knot you, and you're so desperate you seek a puny human?"

He squeezes too hard. My vision darkens and weight presses down on my skull. He pushes my shirt strap off my shoulder and squeezes my right breast as though he has every right. My traitorous body springs to life, hardening my nipples and sending heat through my abdomen. I tear at his wrist and struggle for oxygen as my core morphs into a lake of lava.

"If you need relief, I will give it."

The dark promise in his gravelly voice causes fresh slick to trail down my legs. He pulls in a breath through his nose and smirks. Loosening his grip so I can suck down a ragged breath, he leans down and presses his cheek against my sore face.

"If you need pain, I will give it."

His savage nip to my earlobe stings all the way to my clit. He hooks his elbow under my knee and shoves it against the wall, opening me for him and bending me in half.

"Anything you need, I will be the one to satisfy you."

My eyes roll to the back of my head as he thrusts his humongous shaft into my body. Horrible pleasure-pain barrels through me, my womb contracting in an immediate orgasm. Slick splatters onto the garbage underneath our feet as he shoves more of himself into me. Primed from Sunil's teasing, wrecked from their ruthless fucking, I accept his invasion with both ease and difficulty.

My body wants more, but my mind screams in denial.

The decrepit organ pounding in my chest reaches for his, yearning for the power he holds.

When his semi engorged knot mashes against my folds, my vision blanks to white. I can't breathe through the waves of euphoria smashing through me.

He works his hips back and forth, pummeling my insides until his partially formed knot pushes through the tight ring of my opening. I seize yet again, too far gone for logical thought.

He slides me higher on the wall and fucks up into me, never fully pulling out but jamming in so hard my entire body jerks. His scent envelopes me as I float in clouds of bliss. All my worries sink to the bottom of reality's murky depths.

I want nothing more than to fly among the fluffy white plumes of pleasure he offers. Nothing could make this moment more perfect, except for a monster with purple eyes. My lids blink and for a moment I think I see Sunil over Rajani's shoulder, but my alpha fucks me so hard my eyes lose focus.

Crimson orbs block my vision, the mania emanating from them snapping me out of my stupor.

With one last savage thrust, he fully seats himself and releases a rush of seed as his knot expands.

Agony blasts through my shoulder as he sinks his teeth into my flesh.

CHAPTER EIGHT

Rajani

Nothing has ever felt as amazing as the omega wrapped around me. Bright lights spear through my skull as her flavor hits my tongue, sweet and decadent and too perfect.

Reality snaps into focus.

What the hells have I done?

I wrench my head away from her savaged shoulder and snarl. Reaching between my legs, I pinch my balls to hurt myself, but find my knot already deflating. Confusion, disbelief, and horror drown my lust, cutting my release short. I yank my shaft from her body and peel my hand off her throat. She drops to the ground in a heap of abused, leaking flesh.

Our mixed essences drip from my cock and land in her hair and lap. Her chin lifts and aims vulnerable, wounded brown orbs up at me.

I see myself as the monster I am. Doubt and self-hatred, emotions I've never entertained before, nearly send me to my knees.

I step away from her. Once. Twice.

"What have you done?"

Sunil's voice sounds from far away despite his shoulder brushing against mine.

This is wrong. Backwards. It was my brother who wanted a mate, not me. It was Sunil who fought me for rights to knot her again on this sacred night, not me. I wanted nothing to do with her. I don't want to be tethered to a female.

I should be angry with him, not the other way around.

Her pain spears through my soul from the partial bond between us.

It's too much.

"What are you doing?"

Sunil's accusatory tone barely reaches through my cotton stuffed ears. I turn on my heel and step toward the mouth of the alley.

I must leave, find another female to knot, and forget this ever happened.

I manage three strides before my knees crack against the pavement. Agony pierces my chest, invisible blades sliding between my ribs and puncturing my organs. The unfinished bond threatens to end me. I catch myself on my knuckles before I split my head on the concrete.

Why can't I shift to shadow?

Everything I fear is coming true. Bonding with a human will destroy my powers.

Every cell in my body demands I turn around and close the distance between myself and the omega who bewitched me. I force my muscles onward, pushing through the agony of my soul with stubborn strength. When my shoulders give out, I flop to the concrete and pull myself across the disgusting surface, belly crawling like the worm I am.

"Rajani, stop."

The cotton shoved in my ears makes it easy to ignore my brother's call. If only tamping out my connection with the female was so easy.

I don't know her name. I've never known the names of our sacrifices. I've never needed nor wanted to know.

Not having her name bothers me. I push the weak emotions away and reach for my next handhold.

"Look at me, brother," Sunil says in an eerily calm voice. I can't ignore the note of finality prominent in his tone, so I twist to look over my shoulder.

My heart stops.

He sits with my omega cradled in his lap, one hand stroking her hair from her face with gentle fingers. My gut tightens as I meet his eyes.

He lowers his face to her neck and bites. I watch as his teeth disappear into her flesh.

My agony increases tenfold as his soul blasts mine to pieces, highlighting not only how much my words have wounded him but also how deeply the little female's soul hurts. He ferries her misery into my chest, forcing me to experience everything I put her through. My body moves of its own volition, changing direction and sliding through filth to reach the other parts of my heart.

Dull brown eyes stare up at nothing as Sunil lifts his head away from my omega's throat. She blinks but doesn't react when I touch her shoulder.

Her indifference scares me.

Did we break the one omega we assumed was unbreakable? Did I ruin our chances at a decent life?

She can't stay catatonic forever. If she dies, my brother and I will carry this pain until we fade into the nether.

I can't run away.

She won't forgive me. No one could forgive someone who's done such horrible things to them.

I can't forgive myself. Terrorizing and rutting her felt right, but marking her? The worst mistake in history.

There's no going back.

I rise onto my hip and scoot closer.

We must cement this bond between us, otherwise we'll waste away from heartbreak.

Sunil sticks his nail in a gash I gave him during our bathroom fight and slices it open again. Dark red liquid oozes from his forearm, but when he presses it to her lips, she doesn't respond.

Panic triples my heart rate.

I grab her jaw and pry her lips apart, snarling at the swelling handprint left behind by the human male and growing more desperate as she doesn't react beyond a slight wince. I default to anger.

"She must mark you. Now," I demand in a voice deepened with fury.

Despite the blood trickling past her lips, she stares at the sky and breathes through her nose without moving. When crimson leaks from the corner of her mouth and paints a trail down toward her chin, my control breaks. I roar and grab her, wrapping one hand around her throat and the other in her hair.

She must complete the bond.

I tell myself my desperation is for my brother, but the inner layers of my soul admit the truth.

I want her for myself.

CHAPTER NINE

Sunil

My fist splits open as I knock Rajani to the ground. I shake the ache from my knuckles and check our omega's throat, purring when I find no new marks. I spare my brother a cold and annoyed glance before brushing her hair away from her temples.

"You won't reach her with violence, imbecile," I mumble, fighting through my sense of dread as I glance up from her expressionless face. I don't like how she lies lax in my arms, like a rag doll without a soul.

Rajani surprises me with a look of grief.

"Then how?"

I scoff and trace the delicate features of our partially bonded mate.

"Have you learned nothing these past decades as we watched the humans?"

"I learned plenty," he responds through gritted teeth.

"You learned the wrong things," I snap. The pity I feel for him flees. He had many opportunities to see both good and bad in the human race. Much of what he hates about them reflects himself, if only he weren't too stubborn to see it.

"She needs comfort, kindness, and assurance of our intent."

Silence follows my proclamation.

"How do you know this? And how the hells are we supposed to give her comfort, kindness, and assurance? We're Shadows of Sathanas, for fuck's sake."

I hold in my snarl and caress her ear and throat, careful to avoid the ravaged flesh on her shoulder from my brother's teeth.

"Yes, we are Shadows of Sathanas, but why should that prevent us from adapting? Exploring? Loving?"

"It goes against everything he instilled in us!"

"He made us from his own lack of joy. His own selfishness. Tell me, brother, if he had any use for us, where is he? Where has he been for the last three decades? Why do we fade closer to death despite our loyalty?"

With every word I speak, his brows scrunch tighter until I stop and pry open our brother bond, showing him things he never thought to look for. His brows rise and shock widens his eyes.

"Brother, I... I knew you were curious about the mate bond, but I..." he struggles for a moment, halfway propped up from his fall, searching for the words he means to say. "I didn't realize you spent the last few decades studying and yearning for one."

"Every time I mentioned the subject, you closed yourself off for months. For months, Rajani! We may be creatures of darkness, but we aren't built for solitude. Why do you think Sathanas created us in pairs?"

His silence highlights his understanding.

"I don't think I can give her what she needs."

His quiet answer kicks me in the gut.

"You don't have to. We'll figure it out together."

He watches as my fingers trail down her bruised and filthy arm. When he pushes himself to a full seated position, I expect him to speak, but he brings his knees up and rests his elbows on them. His fingers dive into his short hair and he slumps into himself, a picture of conflicted alpha.

"Have I ever led you down the wrong path?" I prod him. He doesn't move for several seconds.

"No, you haven't. What do we do?" He says to his knees.

"Purr for her. Touch her. Worship her like you did when you cleaned her."

"I didn't."

"Don't lie! You spew lies because you're scared. You hurt her because you're scared. I won't have it!"

"What if that's all I have to give?"

"It isn't. Otherwise, you wouldn't have sunk to your knees and been gentle with her."

"It was a fluke. I don't know why or how I did it."

"It wasn't a fluke. You followed your instincts and treated your future mate with the worship she deserves. You can do it again. You *will* do it again."

"I'll also hurt her again."

I swallow the annoyed growl building in my throat and caress our omega with slow sweeps of my palm.

"She is omega. She needs to hurt, just not like this. Never like this again."

Several heartbeats pass before Rajani lifts his head and glares at me through the darkness.

"You will be her only defense against me."

I grind my jaw and will my heart to stop pounding against my breastbone.

"So be it."

His red eyes peer back at me for another long moment before he drops his gaze to the female lying in my arms. He lowers his knees and leans forward, releasing a resonant purr before tentatively touching her elbow.

Hells, he's a mess. So am I.

She's worse. The will to live drains from her with every second, the incomplete mating bonds too much of a burden for her to bear. I fill my lungs before exhaling and giving her the rumble her soul needs to remain tethered to this realm.

She twitches, but doesn't look away from the sky.

"She's dying."

I ignore my brother's grim tone and shuffle her around until I cradle her head in my hand.

"Keep purring. Come closer."

When Rajani scoots closer without hesitation, I transfer her shoulders to his lap but keep my hand wrapped around the base of her skull.

"Cut your arm," I instruct as I check the wound on my forearm. It trickles blood instead of pouring, already significantly healed.

The trails of crimson running from the corners of her mouth irritate and worry me. She must accept us. Now.

"Put your cut to her mouth."

His arm blocks the lower half of her face as I cup her right breast and rub my thumb over her nipple. It peaks under my digit.

My purr deepens.

"Touch her. Arouse her."

His rumble weaves a cloud of lust around us as he dips down and nuzzles her temple.

"With pleasure," he murmurs against her ear.

I wedge my arm under his, parting her teeth as far as possible and ensuring both our wounds leak straight into her mouth. Rajani ghosts his fingertips down her ribs, brushing the side of my hand as he reaches across her chest and fills his palm with the breast closest to me. Together, we knead and pluck until her nipples turn red and her skin pebbles.

My brother tilts his chin, capturing the lobe of her ear between his teeth, before his fingers wander down her stomach and tease the top of her mound. The erotic sight pulls a moan from me.

Brown orbs shift to mine, the stubborn glint brighter despite the weight of encroaching death. I flex my hand and send a stream of blood onto her tongue. Rajani pushes his fingers between her legs, his control breaking as the fresh scent of her slick perfumes the air, and the lewd sounds of her pussy squelching around his digits drive us higher.

She swallows.

Her entire body gives a vicious jerk. A poignant moment of utter stillness fills me with trepidation. Seizures hit her, contorting her from head to toe, dampening my lust and striking fear into my heart. We pin her to our laps, doing our best to prevent her from injuring herself.

The sound of her heart pounding against her sternum underlies the involuntary gasps and moans as she writhes in agony. Words pass through my numb lips, their meaning escaping me for long, torturous moments as I stare between my brother and our ailing omega.

"Maybe humans and Shadows aren't compatible."

Crimson eyes narrow and determination hardens Rajani's features. He snarls at me before leaning down to threaten our female in a low, urgent voice.

"Don't you dare slip into the afterlife. You will accept our claims. You will submit to our demands. Everything you have belongs to us now. We will not allow your death. Open those striking brown eyes and give me what I need. Give me your anger. Your pain."

Despite her body's contortions, her lids lift and aim blackened orbs at his face. My gut clenches at the juxtaposition of demonic and angelic, her delicate features at odds with the evilness trapped within her eyes.

She shows him the depths of her agony, flicking the bond between them and opening the link until inky black daggers embed themselves into his soul. After a labored breath, his lips tilt in a pleased smirk.

"Such a good, feisty little kitty. More."

I watch in rapt awe as the alpha who, mere moments ago, despaired over his lack of abilities, takes the reins and ushers our omega back to life with his twisted form of control. She rises to his challenge, inundating him with her emotions.

Her body loses its rigidness, easing into a pliant state with intermittent tremors. As they continue their battle, I release her ankle and run my hand up her leg, my purr thickening the closer my fingers get to her drenched pussy. Slick wets my lap and drips to the concrete underneath my ass, the amount alarming. I play in the remnants produced by her body as it accepted our bonds.

Her lids droop and the last of her shaking ends. She takes her first steady breath and swallows before forcing her eyes to focus on Rajani.

"I hate you," she hisses.

Rajani's smile widens.

"Good. Cling to those emotions, little female. You'll need them to survive what we have planned for you."

My cock throbs against her hip, trapped between our bodies at the sensual menace in his tone. She doesn't blush, but her swift inhale broadcasts her needy thoughts. As our minds calm from the height of panic, a sense of tranquility spreads between the three of us.

I bypass her swollen pussy, enjoy the curve of her hip, then trace her side until I reach her jaw. Cupping her chin, I ask what I've wanted to ask since we had her locked on our knots.

"What's your name, little pussycat?"

Her brows scrunch. Rajani leans down and whispers into her ear, "Fight us all you want, tiny female. We'll get what we want, no matter what it takes."

Her forehead creases as she swallows, but she relaxes further, exhaustion making her seem heavier in my lap.

"Jennifer."

Her shoulders slump as she drifts into a sleep so sudden my heart stalls, the only sign she's still alive the moving of her chest. I caress her face and purr for her, enjoying my brother's deeper harmony, letting my emotions play through me as I take stock of her deplorable state. She has too much blood and grime on her, plus the stench of human male clings to her flesh despite our bodies cocooning her away from the world.

Foreboding strikes me half a second before Jennifer's ashen pallor flushes and heat blasts from her skin. Her nipples harden and slick gushes down her thighs. She squeaks and moans in her sleep, exhaustion holding her hostage while lust infects her veins.

Understanding dawns.

"It's still Halloween," I snarl through gritted teeth.

"We're Shadows of Sathanas, bound by The Keeper of Halloween," Rajani rumbles through a tight throat.

"Which means she's now a Halloween omega," I say, fighting the need building in my spine as her scent blossoms.

"And omegas go into heat on their holiday," my brother growls as he cups her swollen breast in his palm.

I meet his stunned expression and speak the words neither of us ever expected to say.

"Our mate is going into heat."

For another moment, we sit frozen in disbelief, but another cramp works through her unconscious body and spurs us into reality.

"To the deepest layers of the darkest hell, how are we supposed to provide for her? We're Shadows. We have no place in this realm, nor The Knottiverse." Panic creeps into my tone.

Rajani studies our omega for a moment before meeting my eyes.

"We do whatever it takes," he says with such fierceness my mania slips away, leaving nothing but determination.

We have each other. We have knowledge and skills mere mortals do not.

And we have her. Jennifer. Our mate.

Chapter Ten

Jennifer

The oddest tinkling sound filters into my right ear through the haze of sleep. Confusion pulls me up from the bowels of darkness, but exhaustion beckons me back. I float in the space between wakefulness and slumber, catching snippets of my surroundings before mist coats me again.

Delicious warmth encompasses my body and seeps into my bones. Sounds become muffled before warm arms lift me into a seated position.

Hard muscles press against my back and masculine thighs spread my own.

Unbearable heat licks through my body, scorching me from head to toe and leaving me a boneless heap. I pry my lids open to get my bearings but close them and moan as amazing scents invade my nostrils.

"Good girl. Let us take care of you."

The words vibrate into my back from Rajani's chest. Water laps at the underside of my breasts. Two purrs lift my troubles away as their rough hands sweep over me. The weird tinkling sound, like water in a tiny, decorative fountain, continues to distract me. I open my eyes and nearly moan as my abdomen clenches in want. Sunil's vibrant purple orbs shine with lust in the candlelight, reflecting the bubbles floating along the top of the water.

Blinking through the crush of need brought on by the visual delight, I breathe in through my nose and lose my battle. A wanton moan escapes from my sore throat, expanding Sunil's pupils until only a sliver of purple remains. His shoulders gleam and steam rises from his hair. I want to lick every inch of him, indescribably jealous of the water clinging to his body.

He lifts his hand to reveal a washcloth, which he strokes over my hairline and dips in the water until all traces of filth are gone. Pleasure darkens his face as his arm brushes the outer curve of my breast.

Lust blasts through me, turning my nipples diamond hard and heightening my senses until my brain threatens to malfunction. He encompasses my needy breasts with his hands, the washcloth between us on one side, and squeezes them as though he has every right.

I groan, wanting more.

Rajani's thick length grinds against my lower back, his left forearm pressing my hips down while his right hand roams my body.

The wave of mindless need fades. Tears sting my eyes.

"What did you do to me?"

"We claimed you."

I narrow my gaze on Sunil's eyes, wanting to stare at his sexy lips, but knowing I won't be able to look away if I do.

"You claimed me? I'm not a possession."

My words prompt a chuckle from my seat. Rajani's fingers tease my inner thigh, perilously close to my aching core. I fight the urge to buck my hips and close the distance.

"You are ours, whether or not you want to be," Rajani says, increasing the need between my legs while stunning me into silence by resting his cheek on the top of my head in an unexpected display of tenderness.

"Which means," Sunil begins, pinching my nipples between his thumb and forefinger before continuing, "that we're yours, too."

He gives me a savage tweak, grinning from ear to ear as I squeak and struggle to raise my hands to protect myself. Rajani holds my arms captive against my sides as he nips my ear.

"Hear that, Jennifer? For what it's worth, you own us. All of us. Body, mind, soul—we're yours."

My insides melt at Rajani's declaration as his breath teases my ear. Sunil plucks my nipples again and caresses the whole of my breasts before spanning his fingers around my ribs and dragging his arms downward.

A raging inferno barrels through me. I can't breathe. My vision dims and my skin turns clammy.

I don't want to die, but death would be a relief.

When my senses return, I sit wrapped in fluffy towels and bracketed by two massive bodies. Something cold presses against my lips. I jerk at the unexpected sensation.

"Drink, tiny kitty," Rajani urges from my right, and without thinking, I open my mouth and accept what he offers. Cool water slides onto my tongue.

Thirst ravages my insides. I struggle to take the glass from him, but their powerful arms keep me bound within the towels. Sunil nuzzles my left temple and murmurs nonsensical, soothing words in my ear. I calm and sip the water, despite wanting to guzzle it.

When the glass pulls away from my lips, I whine and pry my eyelids open. Confusion jumbles my thoughts as I glimpse a high ceiling, modern furnishings, and fancy light fixtures.

I've never been in a room so posh. Even the bedspread and the towels scream high class money. I part my lips to ask where we are, but Sunil pushes food onto my tongue. Tart and sweet, I moan and bite the strawberry like I haven't eaten in a decade, leaning forward and snagging more before he pulls it away. I moan and chew and swallow so fast I almost choke.

More food teases my lips. Bite after bite, morsel after morsel, I eat from their hands as they alternate who feeds me. Different types of cheese, fruits, and bite sized meats slide down my gullet, my stomach hollow until it suddenly threatens to burst.

When Rajani offers me another bite, I turn my head away. His brows scrunch. He rolls onto his hip, blocking out the light and towering over me with a menacing expression.

"Eat."

He thrusts the food against my lips. I clamp my teeth together and shake my head.

Sunil nudges him. His hand moves, but I can't break our eye contact to see what's happening. My stomach clenches and core throbs as his eerie red eyes light with mischief.

Something warm and thick smears across my lips. The moment the scent of chocolate teases my nostrils, I deepen my scowl at him and fight my desires. Saliva floods my mouth and I swallow several times.

He swirls his digit in the mess before dipping his fingertip behind my bottom lip.

I lose the battle, my tongue sweeping out to lick his finger before he pulls away. Rajani moans as I lean forward and take more of his digit into my mouth, lapping at his flesh after I consume the chocolate.

Sunil's chocolate-covered finger slides along the corner of my mouth. I turn my head and grant him access, lost in a wave of heat and longing. Bliss hovers just within reach. Their moans dare me to continue.

I whine when my treats disappear, only to lose myself to thirst when another glass of water appears in front of my face. I drink it as fast as they'll allow.

Too full to move, afraid my stomach will slosh if I shift, I slump against the headboard and let my eyes drift closed.

After what feels like two seconds, heat roars through me. I gasp awake and writhe against silky sheets, the cool air rushing over my naked flesh doing nothing to calm the inferno in my body.

"Hush, little pussycat. You're safe. We're here."

Sunil's words shouldn't be comforting, but a sense of calm slides into my chest. I beat back the instincts demanding I settle into his care and blink until my eyes clear. The thin rings of purple around his blown pupils call to me.

"It's because I'm with you that I'm not safe."

I mean to sound angry, but my words emerge breathy. Rajani's low hum pulls my attention to his red eyes. He smirks before opening his mouth.

"This is going to be fun."

My heart skips a beat as tendrils of fear slip into my chest from his words.

"You're going to hurt me," I breathe, accusation hidden within my needy voice.

"We're going to help you," Sunil insists as he strokes my hair from my face.

I open my mouth to argue, but another wave of heat pummels my insides, resulting in a pain-filled gasp.

"What's wrong with me?"

Sunil tips my chin toward him.

"You're going into heat."

I blink at him, my mind empty for a few seconds before I understand his meaning.

"Like a cat or a dog?"

The moment my words sink in past the lust clouding the room, both alphas smile purely wicked smirks.

"Good thing you had cat ears to lead us to you. Where did they end up?" Sunil asks while he traces a finger down my cheek.

"Under the sink," Rajani responds, surprising me. "I almost took them as a souvenir, except Shadows have no belongings in any realm."

Rajani's words reveal the deep longing in his soul, and my mind latches on to his yearning instead of the implications held within the word *realms*. I know they aren't from Earth, but that doesn't mean I'm ready to contemplate their origins.

My midsection cramps. I wrap my arms around my stomach and curl into a ball on my side. Slick coats my thighs and soaks the bed under my hip. When the pain finally relents, I suck down pheromones-laden air and hold in tears.

"H-how do you help?"

I cling to the last of my strength, afraid another cramp will hit me and suck me into oblivion.

"We knot you," Sunil says, his voice guttural and much too far away. Every cell in my body begs for him to touch me.

"Then do it. I can't handle this anymore."

"You've barely begun, little omega."

Rajani's words pull the first tear from my eye. It slips down to the soft sheet under my head.

"Don't torture me, Rajani. I *hurt*."

The mattress dips and thick fingers trace down my spine as he morphs his purr into a song of comfort. The worst of my pain eases, carried away by two masculine rumbles.

"Say it again," Rajani demands, his lips hovering above my ear as he looms over my back.

"I hurt," I whimper, my insides throbbing.

"No. My name. Say my name again."

A sob wracks my chest, hitting me out of nowhere. I fight for control, but another bout of pain consumes my stomach. Agony slices into my guts, stealing my senses.

Their hands caress my arms and legs, avoiding my erogenous zones.

I cry as the pain fades, leaving me to lie like a lump of jelly on the bed.

"Help me, Rajani."

Rajani's massive hand grabs my chin and turns my face to his before his lips descend. His tongue invades my mouth, wiping away all traces of angst and building a more natural desire. As dark relief pulses through my veins, I sigh and flick my tongue against his. He moans and yanks himself away.

I blink in shock, unable to process the void in front of me while his taste still lingers in my mouth. His grip on my chin tilts my face toward purple eyes.

Hunger shines from Sunil's features, but so does a patience so profound I decide to never push him again. Where Rajani may be rash and brutal, Sunil's temperament oozes wisdom and lethal understanding. Testing his resolve will no doubt leave me so emotionally raw I may never heal.

Words slip from my lips, so honestly my throat tightens and more salty liquid drips from my eyes.

"Please help me, Sunil. I want you."

Pleasure washes over his features. He braces his knee on the mattress and leans over to take my mouth in a kiss so thorough I forget to breathe.

I tremble in confusion as he backs away, both men leaving me to lie alone on the massive bed.

Are they rejecting me?

White-hot agony lances into my stomach. Slick soaks the mattress. My hands claw at the soft bedding, destroying any semblance of order.

I need to fix it.

A fuzzy blanket lands on my legs.

"Wha—"

"Nest, Jennifer," Sunil interrupts me with his demand, never ceasing his purr.

Instincts take over, hijacking my brain and moving my body. I yank the new blanket to my face and snarl at the chemical smell.

Quilts, sheets, and pillows land on the mattress. Each one smells horrible.

I snarl and push the pile off the bed. Masculine arms dump the fabrics back onto the mattress, but I immediately push them off.

Rajani weaves his fingers into my hair and yanks my face up to his. He scowls, but Sunil's voice breaks the tension between us.

"What's wrong, little pussycat?"

"They stink."

The fury leaks from Rajani's features and a smile creeps onto his face.

"We can fix that. Watch us, tiny female. I want to feel your eyes on me while I prepare your nesting materials."

Dark tendrils of desire thicken my blood as my mates choose their first offering. They rub the fabrics over their entire body, paying special attention to the cocks jutting from their hips.

I want to touch and taste them so badly I crawl closer without meaning to, but Sunil tosses his blanket at me before I reach the edge of the mattress.

Bliss. Almost utter perfection. If only it held both my alphas' pheromones.

My hands knead the fabric into the mattress, fluffing and primping and moving on autopilot.

Another blanket joins the first. Then a pillow. Then two more blankets. More bedding drops onto the mattress, each piece different from the last. Firm pillows, fluffy clouds, fuzzy blankets, thick quilts. I use everything tossed my way, instincts guiding me to make the space as comfortable as possible.

I don't understand why this weighs so heavy on my heart, but each piece must fit exactly where I want it, so I push and pull until satisfaction flows through my veins.

"She's too fucking gorgeous. Look at her aura shine, brother," Sunil rumbles from the foot of the bed.

"Too perfect," Rajani growls.

I crawl to the footboard and stick my head out of my cocoon. Two very erect, very large cocks greet me. I reach forward, but Sunil's fingers wrap around my wrist and halt my momentum.

"Your nest is sacred. Invite us in," Sunil demands.

"Nest?" My lust-drunk brain refuses to understand. Rajani responds, his rocky words tumbling through my abdomen.

"Yes, your nest is perfect. You built a safe, comfortable place to accept us during your estrous. Now, invite us in before we drag you out and mount you on the floor."

I glance beyond their legs at the pristine white carpet.

"Where are we, anyway?"

"A house."

Rajani's curt response makes me pause, but I force myself to ask my next question.

"Your house?"

"No."

"Then... did you rent it?"

They each cock a brow, answering me without words.

"Oh no, what did you do? Are we trespassing?"

"No. The homeowners know we're here," Sunil growls.

"Did you hurt them?"

Rajani tilts his head. Dread settles in my gut. Sunil speaks, not allaying my fears but wiping away the worst of my worry.

"We scared them, but we didn't touch them. They won't be back for a while."

"What if they call the cops?"

"That won't happen," Rajani replies. I stare at them, praying for a sign that they're joking.

Of course, they aren't. Another blast of agony stabs into my stomach. I decide I don't care what they did to make sure we have a safe place to end this agony.

Light bounces off something in the corner. I lean and look around the wall of man flesh and find a massive mound of empty plastic packaging.

"Did you..." I gulp, knowing the answer but needing to ask anyway, "did you buy the new bedding?"

Rajani's teeth shine in the low lighting as he smirks at me.

"If you're worried about petty theft, then you truly don't want to know how we acquired this house for the next few weeks."

My eyes widen at his words.

"The next few weeks?"

"This is your first heat, so yes, our knots may be locked inside you for weeks on end."

My head spins and a floaty sensation hits me.

I won't survive this.

A wave of heat powers through me. Sweat and tears coat my clammy skin. I reach for my only source of relief.

Both males hiss as I grab their shafts, but neither steps forward when I tug.

"Invite us in, little pussycat," Sunil urges, his tone both playful and desperate.

"Please, Rajani. Please, Sunil. Get in my nest."

The heady scent of thunderstorms invades my sinuses as they crawl into my cocoon and wedge me between them. Their callused hands explore every inch of me until arousal consumes my every thought.

I give myself to them, at first to find release, but as they master my body, I forget to shield my heart. They flex their might within our bonds, stretching my soul as they rearrange my insides with their knots.

I'll never be alone ever again. Sunil will forever push my endurance while Rajani will ensure every dark, depraved fantasy I have finds fulfillment.

What this means exactly for our day-to-day future, I don't know, but lying trapped on their knots and cocooned away from the world by their massive bodies, I find I don't care.

Nothing matters except the here and now. Nothing exists beyond my Shadows and their shafts lodged within my body.

I need only their hearts woven within mine.

Forever.

***

Need more dark and filthy omegaverse?

Join my Newsletter by scanning the QR code below or visit:

https://vtbonds.com/newslettersubscriber/

***

Want to tell me you love me? Leave a review!

KEEP UP WITH V.T. BONDS

My Newsletter:

https://vtbonds.com/newslettersubscriber/

My website:

https://vtbonds.com/

Find me on:

Bookbub

Goodreads

Facebook

www.ingramcontent.com/pod-product-compliance
Ingram Content Group UK Ltd.
Pitfield, Milton Keynes, MK11 3LW, UK
UKHW021647190726
13853UKWH00001B/118